STERLING CHILDREN'S BOOKS
New York

An Imprint of Sterling Publishing
387 Park Avenue South
New York, NY 10016

Text © 2014 by Phillis Gershator
Illustrations © 2014 by David Walker

ISBN 978-1-4549-1032-9

Library of Congress Cataloging-in-Publication Data

Gershator, Phillis.
  Time for a bath / by Phillis Gershator ; illustrated by David Walker.
      pages cm
  Summary: No matter what kind of messes a little bunny experiences through the day, bath time makes things fresh and new.
  ISBN 978-1-4549-1032-9
  [1. Stories in rhyme. 2. Baths--Fiction. 3. Rabbits--Fiction.] I. Walker, David, 1965- illustrator. II. Title.
  PZ8.3.G3235Ths 2012
  [E]--dc23
                          2013030256

Distributed in Canada by Sterling Publishing
c/o Canadian Manda Group, 165 Dufferin Street
Toronto, Ontario, Canada M6K 3H6
Distributed in the United Kingdom by GMC Distribution Services
Castle Place, 166 High Street, Lewes, East Sussex, England BN7 1XU
Distributed in Australia by Capricorn Link (Australia) Pty. Ltd.
P.O. Box 704, Windsor, NSW 2756, Australia

Designed by Andrea Miller

For information about custom editions, special sales, and premium and corporate purchases,
please contact Sterling Special Sales at 800-805-5489 or specialsales@sterlingpublishing.com.

Manufactured in China
Lot #:
2 4 6 8 10 9 7 5 3 1
07/14

www.sterlingpublishing.com/kids

TIME
for a
BATH

by Phillis Gershator

illustrated by David Walker

STERLING CHILDREN'S BOOKS

New York

Rise and shine!

We'll work and play
all year long
and every day.

OOPS! A mess,
but that's okay.

Spills and spatters,
goop and grit.

Fill the tub—
What time is it?

Hop in and then,
rub-a-dub-dub,
all clean again.

Look for earthworms,

track the ants,

roll around
in grassy pants.

Dig a hole,

plant a pit,

water and weed—
What time is it?

Time for a bath!

Splash and squirt.
Rub-a-dub-dub.
Good-bye, dirt.

Hunt for crabs,

run to and fro,

take sand home
between each toe.

Share a **big**
banana split.
Drippy, sweet—

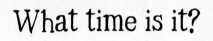

What time is it?

Time for a bath!

Quick, quick—undress.
Rub-a-dub-dub,
no more mess.

Swing and slide,

hang upside down,

chase the leaves,
red, yellow, brown.

Pick a puddly place to sit,
make a pie—
What time is it?

Time for a bath!

Here we go.
Rub-a-dub-dub
from head to toe.

Paint a picture,
play with clay.
Be an artist
every day.

Uh oh!
Got wet,
a little bit.
An accident . . .

What time is it?

Time for a bath!

A shampoo, too,
with rainbow bubbles,
pink, green, blue.

BUNNY
BUBBLES

Splish splash splosh!
Can everybody fit?
Duck, fish, whale—

What time is it?

The best time,
bath time,
time with you.
All clean again,
all fresh and new.

Wrapped in a towel,
warm and dry,
ready for a story
and a lullaby.

And when we say,

"Sweet dreams, sleep tight,"

we hug and cuddle
and kiss good night.